GOODNIGHT
TIGER

Timothy Knapman · Laura Hughes

LITTLE TIGER PRESS
London

It was the middle of the night,
but **Emily** couldn't sleep . . .

because of all the
BELLOWING
and STOMPING

and TRUMPETING
and GROWLING!

"The **animals** must have escaped from the **ZOO!**" she cried.

But there was no one in the street except next door's cat.

Emily looked **under** the bed,

on **top** of the wardrobe,

and through **all** her toys and clothes,

until at last she saw that the **noise** was coming from . . .

. . . the **animals** in her wallpaper!

The gorilla

BELLOWED

and the hippo STOMPED

and the elephant

TRUMPETED

and the tiger

GROWLED

until Emily shouted,

"Go t

sleep!"

"We've tried and tried but we **can't!**"
said the tiger.

"We'll soon see about that,"
said Emily.

And she grabbed a chair

and **climbed** up

into the jungly wallpaper.

"Have you had your **bath** yet?"
asked Emily.

"No," said the tiger.

"Well **no wonder**
    you can't sleep!" said Emily.

But there wasn't a bath in the **whole** of the jungle.
"We could always use the watering hole,"
said the tiger.

The hippo scrubbed
behind his ears.

The elephant used his trunk
to give himself a shower.

The gorilla shampooed his fur
till it was soft and shiny . . .

But when the tiger jumped in,
he landed on the crocodiles!
What a RUMPUS!

SNAP!

"A bath like **that** won't help you get to sleep," said Emily.
"How about some **hot chocolate?**"

"Yes please!"
said the tiger.

But there was no hot chocolate in the **whole** of the jungle.
"We could always use mud," said the tiger.

The gorilla mixed it
very carefully.

And the elephant used his trunk
to pour it into little cups.

It smelt **horrible.**

But when Emily and the tiger drank it,
they found that it **actually** tasted . . .

"A drink like **that** won't help you
get to sleep," said Emily. "But what else can I do?"

Emily tried **everything.**
She gave them a bear to cuddle . . .

but the bear got cross and ran away.

She started to sing them a lullaby, but the whole of the jungle joined in, and it got too

LOUD!

She even tried to turn the lights off,
but she couldn't find a switch **anywhere**.

"And we're
STILL not tired!"
said the animals.

"I don't know what to do!" cried Emily at last.
"**You** can't sleep, and that means
I can't sleep, and I'm

EXHAUSTED!"

"Is there nothing else we can try?"
asked the tiger.

And then Emily had a **wonderful** idea.

"We can have a
bedtime story!"
she said.

"Yes please!" cried the animals.
"We've never had a bedtime story!"

So she told them a story about some animals
who escaped from a zoo, the little girl who found them,
and the **great adventure** they had before
they all went home to bed.

When she was finished,
the gorilla, the hippo
and the elephant
were **fast asleep.**

Emily yawned.
"I'm still wide awake," she said.

"How about a **goodnight snuggle?**" said the tiger.

"Yes please!"
said Emily.

"Goodnight, Emily."
"Goodnight, Tiger."

The next morning when Emily woke up,
the animals were smiling down at
her from the wallpaper.
All except the **tiger**.

Emily found him snuggled up on her bed.
And he was **still** fast asleep.